TRIPLET TROUBLE

and

the Cookie Contest

There are more books about
the Tucker Triplets!

TRIPLET TROUBLE

and

the Cookie Contest

by Debbie Dadey and Marcia Thornton Jones
Illustrated by John Speirs

A
LITTLE APPLE
PAPERBACK

SCHOLASTIC INC.
New York Toronto London Auckland Sydney

In memory of Arthur F. Bailey — DD

To Catherine Nacke Kuhljuergen for fill-ing her cookie jar with homemade sugar cookies made especially for her grand-children. — MTJ

ISBN 0-590-90728-X

Text copyright © 1996 by Debra S. Dadey and Marcia Thornton Jones.
Illustrations copyright © 1996 by Scholastic Inc.
All rights reserved. Published by Scholastic Inc.
LITTLE APPLE and the LITTLE APPLE logo are trademarks of Scholastic Inc.

12 11 10 9 8 7 6 5 4   8 9/9 0 1/0

Printed in the U.S.A.   40

First Scholastic printing, October 1996

Contents

1

Triplet Trouble

Alex Tucker sat down on the grass in front of the Oakridge Retirement Home. She scraped up red and gold leaves until they covered her. All that was showing was her nose.

I sat down beside Alex and picked up a red leaf. My name is Sam Johnson. The Tucker Triplets and I always stop on our way home from school to wave to Miss Crankshaw at 3:15.

Miss Crankshaw was our favorite neighbor when she lived on our street. We would sit on her front porch and she'd tell us stories about life in the old days. She made yummy cookies, too. But then she hurt her hip and had to move into the Oakridge Retirement Home. The Oakridge Retirement Home doesn't allow children in without an adult, so we don't get to talk with Miss Crankshaw very often. Now her nephew lives in her old house with his family.

I looked at my watch. It was only 3:10. It would be another five minutes until Miss Crankshaw came to the window.

Usually, five minutes isn't very long. But when Alex is around, a five-minute wait seems like forever.

Alex Tucker is my best friend. Being with her is fun. Except when we have to wait. Alex doesn't like to wait.

Alex suddenly popped up from the ground. Leaves scattered in every direction. Some even landed on top of Ashley's hair.

"Stop that!" Ashley squealed, plucking a leaf from her blonde ponytail. Ashley Tucker is Alex's sister. Even though they look alike, they are very different. Ashley likes to look perfect all the time.

Alex looked at Ashley. Then her eyes got big and round. I knew what that meant.

It meant Alex was thinking up one of her horrible brilliant ideas. Alex snapped her fingers right in front of her nose.

"These leaves are too pretty to waste," Alex said. "We should decorate with them."

"You can't use leaves to decorate," Adam said. "They crumble and fall apart."

Adam is Ashley and Alex's brother. He is very smart. The Tucker Triplets have the same birthday and the same color hair, but they never ever agree on the same things.

Alex stuck out her chin. "We CAN use leaves and I'll show you," she said.

Alex hunted through the pile of leaves on the ground until she found five bright yellow and orange leaves. First she stuck two through the rubber bands of her short pigtails. The leaves stuck straight out above her ears. Next, she poked leaves into the buttonholes on her sweater. Then she gathered more leaves and poked them into the holes of her sneakers. When she was finished she grinned so big I could see where her front tooth used to be.

"How do I look?" Alex asked.

"You look like a dead tree," Ashley giggled.

I thought so, too. But I didn't want to tell Alex. That would just make her mad. When Alex gets mad, there's always trouble.

"I do not," Alex said. "Tell them, Sam."

Adam, Alex, and Ashley looked at me. I looked at them. I swallowed hard. I liked the Tuckers, but when they put me in the middle of their fights there's bound to be trouble. Triplet Trouble.

2

Homecoming

Just then, Miss Crankshaw knocked on the window. I looked at my watch. It was exactly 3:15! We waved, but Miss Crankshaw didn't wave back. Instead, she opened the big front door to the Oakridge Retirement Home.

We ran up the sidewalk to give her a big hug. She didn't even mind when two of

Alex's leaves stuck to her furry sweater.

"I have great news," Miss Crankshaw said. "I am coming home with my nephew for a visit!"

Ashley cheered and Adam clapped. Alex jumped up and down.

"When?" I asked.

"Tomorrow!" she said with a smile.

"Yay!" we cheered. It would be nice to listen to Miss Crankshaw's stories again and eat her yummy cookies.

For the first time ever, the Tucker Triplets agreed on something. Having Miss Crankshaw home was going to be terrific!

We knew what we had to do. I raced home to get paint, markers, and my dad's saxophone. Then I ran to the Tuckers' house. My dog Cleo followed me.

The Tuckers were in their basement. They had a pile of old paper grocery bags. We cut the bags apart and turned them over.

Adam wrote the letters and Ashley and I painted pictures. Alex plucked leaves from her sweater and glued them on our signs. We cut and painted and glued. Finally, we were finished.

We got up extra early the next morning so we could decorate Miss Crankshaw's yard with our signs. We tied signs to the trees. We taped some on the windows. There were signs everywhere. They all said, WELCOME HOME!

When Miss Crankshaw rode up in her nephew's big blue car, Ashley did a cheer and Adam juggled three balls. I played my saxophone extra loud so Miss Crankshaw would know how glad I was that she was home. Cleo even tried to sing along.

Alex stood on the top step of the porch. She was decorated to match the signs we

had made. She had leaves tied to her pigtails and leaves taped all over her sweatshirt. A WELCOME HOME sign was even
wrapped around her waist. We all got quiet
when Miss Crankshaw walked to the
porch. We wanted her to hear Alex's
speech.

Alex stood up tall and spoke in her most grown-up voice. "The Tucker Triplets and Sam Johnson are pleased to welcome the most bestest neighbor, Miss Crankshaw."

Miss Crankshaw smiled. "This is the most bestest homecoming in the world," she said.

"Just wait until tomorrow. Things will really be cooking!" Alex said and smiled so big you could see where her tooth used to be. Then her eyes got big and she snapped her fingers in front of her nose.

I wasn't sure what Alex was talking about, but I was afraid it was going to be trouble!

3

Burnt Cookies

The next day at school our teacher Mr. Parker held up a sign. In big blue letters it said:

SPELLING TEST

I started to groan, but I didn't. I didn't want to be rude. Alex didn't care. She groaned really loud.

Mr. Parker stared at Alex for a minute. Alex stopped groaning and played with one of the leaves in her hair.

"Now, I have a list of words for you to learn to spell by Friday," Mr. Parker said with a big smile.

I looked around the room. Mr. Parker was the only one smiling. I guess no one else thought a spelling test was funny.

"Don't worry," Mr. Parker said as he passed out the list. "I'm sure you can already spell many of the words."

I looked at the list. Maybe this test wouldn't be so bad. I did know most of the words: cook, book, look, hook, nook, shook, took, and a bunch of other words with two o's in them. The last two were terribly hard: *Halloween* and *October*. I didn't know if I could ever learn those.

Adam Tucker sits in the seat next to me. After he looked at the list, he started smiling just like Mr. Parker. Adam is so smart, he probably already knew how to spell *Halloween*.

Alex looked at the list and started smiling, too. I'm sure Alex didn't know how to spell *Halloween*. Why was she smiling?

"I know how to spell *cook*," Alex

bragged. "As a matter of fact, after today, I'll be the best cook in the world!"

"Why is that?" a girl named Maria asked.

"Because Miss Crankshaw is going to show me how to bake cookies today," Alex announced with a big smile.

"That's not fair," Ashley said. "I have ballet after school. I want to make cookies."

"Me, too," Adam complained. "But Sam and I are going to Randy's house."

"Don't worry," Alex said. "I'll save you some cookies to eat."

Randy rolled his wheelchair up beside Alex. "Maybe Mr. Parker should add the word *cookie* to the spelling test."

I looked up at Mr. Parker. I hoped he wouldn't add any more words. There were already too many for me.

Mr. Parker rubbed his chin and looked at Alex. "Perhaps Alex will bring cookies for the whole class."

"I bet the only cookies you make are

burnt ones," another girl named Barbara teased.

"That's not true!" Alex snapped. "I'll make the best cookies ever. Just wait until tomorrow! You'll see!"

4

Mess

"What a mess!" Ashley said when we walked into Miss Crankshaw's house. Adam, Ashley, and I couldn't believe it. School had been out for two hours. In that time, Alex had destroyed Miss Crankshaw's kitchen.

Brown blobs dripped from the counter to the floor. Sugar sprinkled the floor,

along with a broken egg. Miss Crankshaw and Alex looked like ghosts. Flour covered their aprons and cheeks. Alex even had flour in her hair, along with red and orange leaves.

"You're just in time," Alex said as a buzzer went off. "The first batch is done."

"Yum," I said when I bit into the warm sugar cookie. It was the best cookie I'd ever had.

"These cookies are worth the mess," Adam agreed.

Miss Crankshaw looked around her kitchen. For a minute, I thought she was going to faint. "Oh, my," she said. "I didn't realize it was this bad."

"Don't worry," Alex said. "We'll help you clean up."

"We?" Ashley said. "You're the one who made the cookies."

Alex held up the plate of cookies. "But you're going to help me eat them. Aren't you?"

Adam, Ashley, and I nodded and wiped off the counter. Alex rubbed the egg around on the floor with a paper towel.

Then Miss Crankshaw handed Alex the big plate of cookies.

"I'll finish cleaning," Miss Crankshaw told us. She looked at Alex and said, "I think you're ready to make cookies at your own house. I'm sure they'll be quite good."

Alex smiled and hugged Miss Crankshaw. "Thanks," Alex told her. "I had a lot of fun."

Miss Crankshaw patted Alex on the head. A little puff of flour floated up from Alex's hair. "Enjoy the cookies," Miss Crankshaw told us as she shut the door.

Alex put the plate down on Miss Crankshaw's porch. We all sat down and ate more cookies. "These are sooooo good!" Ashley said.

"Cleo thinks so, too," Adam said. We looked down to see my dog Cleo stealing two cookies off the plate.

"Quit that!" Ashley screamed. Then she sneezed and Cleo ran around the corner of the house. Ashley always sneezes when she's near Cleo.

"You didn't have to yell at Cleo," Alex said. Alex likes Cleo almost as much as I do.

"But the cookies are almost gone," Ashley said.

Alex held up the plate. It was true. Only two cookies were left. "Don't worry," Alex said. "I can make more."

"These cookies are good because Miss Crankshaw helped," Adam said. "Your cookies will probably taste like mud pies."

I didn't want to make Alex mad. But I was afraid Adam was right. Any cookies Alex could make were bound to be terrible.

5

Cookie Cook-Off

We were still sitting on Miss Crankshaw's porch. Alex stuck out her chin. Ashley crossed her arms over her chest. Adam pressed his lips together until they turned into a thin line. Nobody said a word. Sometimes quiet is good, but not when the triplets are around. This kind of quiet meant trouble.

We all looked at the two tiny cookies left on the plate. "I get the rest of the cookies," Alex said. "After all, I helped make them."

"No fair," Ashley said. "I would have helped, but I had my ballet lesson."

"You knew that we couldn't go after school today," Adam added.

Sharing two cookies between the Tucker Triplets was going to be hard. Sharing was one thing they weren't very good at.

"You should have waited until we could help," Ashley told Alex. "Then there would be more cookies for all of us."

"And we'd all know how to make more," Adam said.

Alex put her hands on her hips. "I know how to make more. I watched Miss

Crankshaw. I know her cookie secrets."

Ashley shook her head. "No, you'd get it all wrong. You always get things wrong."

Then Alex's eyes got big. I could tell she was thinking hard. Suddenly, she snapped her fingers in front of her nose. "I'll prove I can make the world's best cookies," she said.

"How?" Ashley asked.

"By baking some right now," Alex said. When she stood up, two leaves floated from her sweatshirt and landed on the ground by her sneakers.

"You can't make cookies by yourself," Ashley told her. "I'd better help you."

Alex put her hands on her hips. "I can make the best cookies you ever tasted all by myself. I learned how while you were off dancing on your tippy-toes."

Ashley stood up to argue but Adam jumped between them.

"I bet my cookies would be better than yours," Adam snapped. "You don't even know how to read a recipe!"

"I know how we can find out," Alex said, but I didn't like the sound of her voice. It sounded as sweet as Miss Crankshaw's cookies.

"How?" Ashley and Adam asked.

"We'll have a cookie cook-off!" Alex said with a grin.

"What's that?" Adam asked.

"A contest," Alex explained. "And the best cookie wins!"

"A contest?" Adam asked. "Mine would win. I always win."

"Not this time," Alex said. "And I'll prove it!" Alex hopped off Miss Crankshaw's porch and ran next door to her house. The door slammed extra hard as she rushed inside.

Adam and Ashley pushed each other trying to get through the door next. The door slammed after them.

The Tucker Triplets are my best friends. They are usually lots of fun. But not when they start daring each other. Then they're nothing but trouble. One thing is for sure, though — triplet trouble can be fun to watch. So I shrugged and followed them inside.

6

Too Many Cooks

Adam and Ashley opened all the kitchen
cabinets until they found their mom's
cookbooks. Then they pulled every one
onto the floor in a big pile.

"Why are you doing that?" Alex asked.

"We need a recipe," Adam explained.

"No, we don't." Alex shook her head.

"Of course we do," Ashley said.

"How else will we know how much sugar to put in?" Adam asked.

"I know," Alex said with a grin. "The more the better!" Alex took a bag of sugar and dumped it into a bowl.

Adam jumped up from the floor. "You don't get all the sugar!" he yelled. "You have to share."

Then he tugged at the bowl. So did Alex. That's when most of the sugar flew out of the bowl and landed in Ashley's hair.

"Quit that!" Ashley squealed.

"Ashley's right," Alex said. "We're wasting sugar. And we need lots of sugar. We also need flour and butter and eggs."

"And salt," Ashley said. "It's all here in this recipe I found."

Adam and Ashley crowded over the cookbook to read the directions. Not Alex. She dumped flour into the bowl with the sugar. She took a wooden spoon and stirred so hard a leaf in her ponytail jiggled loose. Alex didn't notice when it landed in her cookie batter.

Alex grabbed some eggs from the refrigerator. When she did, two eggs slipped out of her hands. Yellow sticky stuff splattered and oozed across the floor.

Adam and Ashley jumped over the mess and started mixing their own bowls of batter. Only theirs didn't look much better than Alex's. All of their bowls were filled with lumpy batter that looked like the clay Mr. Parker keeps for art class.

"We'd better get Mom to help us with the oven," Ashley said.

"These will taste great when they're hot," Alex said.

"Maybe," Adam mumbled. Only he didn't sound very sure.

I knew one thing for sure. Mrs. Tucker wasn't going to be very happy about the cookie contest. I looked around the kitchen. Sugar and flour coated the cabinets and crunched under my sneakers. Butter and egg blobs speckled the floor. It looked like a cookie bomb had exploded right in the middle of Mrs. Tucker's kitchen. Just then I heard footsteps coming down the stairs. It was bound to be Mrs. Tucker.

"I'd better do my homework, now," I told the Triplets.

I didn't wait for them to argue. I hurried out the back door and grabbed Cleo before Mrs. Tucker caught me in the middle of the Tucker Triplets' cookie contest mess.

7

Green

The next morning I carried a plate of chocolate chip cookies into Mr. Parker's classroom. I was proud of them. My dad helped me bake them. He said they were the best he'd ever tasted. Of course, he never had any of Miss Crankshaw's cookies. Her cookies never had burnt edges like mine.

Alex, Adam, and Ashley each had

plates on their desks. "Hi, Sam!" Alex called. "Want to taste my cookies?"

"SHHH!" Ashley said, pointing to the front of the room. Mr. Parker had a big red sign hanging on the board. It had white letters that said: DEAR TIME. I knew that stood for **D**rop **E**verything **A**nd **R**ead.

I grabbed two books from the reading corner and sat down. My cookies could wait until after reading.

While I was reading I smelled something funny. I think it was coming from Alex's cookies. They smelled rotten! And they were green!

Finally Mr. Parker rang the little bell on his desk. Reading time was over. Alex raced up to Mr. Parker's desk with her cookies. Adam and Ashley were right behind her with their plates. I didn't want to be left out. I took my cookies and sat them in front of Mr. Parker.

"What lovely cookies," Mr. Parker said. "Is it someone's birthday?"

"No," Alex said. "It's a contest."

"A cookie contest," Adam told him.

"We'd like you to be the judge," Ashley said. "Which cookies are the best?"

"I'm sure they're all good," Mr. Parker said.

"Try them," Alex said.

Mr. Parker picked up a cookie from Ashley's plate. It crumbled in his hand.

Mr. Parker took a bite and smiled.

"Try mine," Adam said, shoving his plate toward Mr. Parker. Adam's cookies looked good. But when Mr. Parker bit into one, his face turned green. Green like Alex's cookies. Maybe Adam's cookies weren't so good after all.

"Very interesting," Mr. Parker said, "but perhaps we should get to work."

"No," Alex said. "You still have to taste these cookies."

Mr. Parker looked at Alex's green cookies and my crispy cookies. I had the feeling Mr. Parker was putting an end to the cookie contest.

8

Missing

"You have to try my cookies," Alex said loudly. "I colored them green."

"I put chocolate chips in these," I told Mr. Parker.

"Mine are still better," Adam said.

Ashley stomped her foot. "Mine are the best."

"Mine are!" Alex shouted.

Mr. Parker held up his hand. Without a word he tasted Alex's cookies and then mine. He smiled and then wrote a word on a paper. He held it up. In blue letters it said: MISSING.

That word wasn't on our spelling list. I was sounding it out when Adam said, "That says miss-ing."

Mr. Parker nodded. "All your cookies are good in their own way, but something is missing."

"I put in what I was supposed to," Ashley said. "Flour, water, eggs . . ."

"And extra salt," Adam said.

Alex nodded. "I put in lots of sugar and green food coloring."

"My dad helped me read the recipe," I told Mr. Parker. "We put in everything."

Mr. Parker stood up. "All those things are important," he said, "but the most important part is still missing."

"What's that?" Alex asked.

Mr. Parker went to the chalkboard and wrote down a long word. It looked like this: FRIENDSHIP.

Adam, Alex, Ashley, and I stared at the word. Before we could figure it out, Maria stood up. "I know that word," she said. "That's friend-ship. It means being friends."

Alex put her hands on her hips. "You don't need friendship to make cookies."

Mr. Parker circled the word on the board. "Friendship is very important. When it's missing, nothing can be very good."

"Maybe that's why Miss Crankshaw's cookies are so good," Alex said. "Because she is our friend."

"Next time, we'll make the cookies together," Ashley said.

"That's exactly what I planned," Mr. Parker said with a smile. Then he scribbled on a piece of paper with a marker. When he held up his new sign we all cheered. In bright pink letters it said: COOKIE MATH.

We spent the morning helping each other measure butter and flour and stirring sticky batter. Then we had to wait for the cookies to bake.

"Are you ready to taste your math lesson?" Mr. Parker finally asked.

"What if we did something wrong?" Randy asked. "They might taste terrible!"

Alex shook her head. "We know we did everything right," she said, "because we were helping each other."

Then Alex grabbed a cookie and popped it into her mouth. We all watched her chew. Finally she swallowed. Alex smiled so big we could see where her tooth used to be.

Everyone laughed and took a cookie. They were good! I smiled at my friends. I think we all won the cookie contest!

55